JULIE BROWN
RACING AGAINST THE WORLD

The Women of Our Time® series

JULIE BROWN
RACING AGAINST THE WORLD

BY R. R. KNUDSON

Illustrated by J. Brian Pinkney

VIKING KESTREL

For Marilyn Alguire Brown,
to whom any athlete would be proud
to say "Hi, Mom."   R.R.K.

VIKING KESTREL
Published by the Penguin Group
Viking Penguin Inc., 40 West 23rd Street, New York, New York 10010, U.S.A.
Penguin Books Ltd, 27 Wrights Lane, London W8 5TZ, England
Penguin Books Australia Ltd, Ringwood, Victoria, Australia
Penguin Books Canada Ltd, 2801 John Street, Markham, Ontario, Canada L3R 1B4
Penguin Books (N.Z.) Ltd, 182-190 Wairau Road, Auckland 10, New Zealand

Penguin Books Ltd, Registered Offices: Harmondsworth, Middlesex, England

First published in 1988 by Viking Penguin Inc.
Published simultaneously in Canada
1   3   5   7   9   10   8   6   4   2
Text copyright © R.R. Knudson, 1988
Illustrations copyright © J. Brian Pinkney, 1988
All rights reserved
WOMEN OF OUR TIME® is a registered trademark of Viking Penguin Inc.

Library of Congress Cataloging in Publication Data
Knudson, R. Rozanne,   Julie Brown : racing with the world
by R.R. Knudson ;
illustrated—J. Brian Pinkney.
p.   cm.—(Women of our time)
Summary: A biography emphasizing the running career of the woman
who overcame many personal and professional hurdles to compete as a
marathon runner in the 1984 Olympic Games.
ISBN 0-670-81487-3
1. Brown, Julie—Juvenile literature.   2. Runners (Sports)—United
States—Biography—Juvenile literature.   3. Marathon running—
Juvenile literature.   [1. Brown, Julie.   2. Runners (Sports)
3. Marathon running.]   I. Pinkney, J. Brian, ill.   II. Title.
III. Series.   GV1061.15.B76K58   1988   796.4'26—dc19
[B]   [92]   88-17343   CIP

Printed in the United States of America by Haddon Craftsmen, Bloomsburg, Pennsylvania
Set in Garamond #3.

May 03, '89
j GV 1061
.15
.B76 K58/88

CONTENTS

JULIE BROWN
RACING AGAINST THE WORLD

1

Under the Big Sky

Summers are hot and dry in central Montana—grand times for riding horses. On Saturdays whole families mount up to wander through the countryside.

Farm and ranch lands spread in every direction. There are few trees to block the views. Wildlife can be seen close up: jackrabbits and coyotes, prairie dogs and hawks. Gentle foothills invite riders to climb for a wider look at the Yellowstone River. Way off in the distance are mountains covered with evergreens. They appear deep blue against an endless sky.

Julie Brown was born in the center of this scenery—Billings, Montana—on February 4, 1955. She was the third child of Marilyn Alguire Brown and Rockwood Brown, and it wasn't long before her dad put Julie up on a horse so she could ride out with her brother Scott and sister Holly.

"Julie didn't balk," her mom says about that first ride. "She took to horses like a duck to water."

She took to swimming, boating, hiking, and running as easily, as fearlessly.

Each summer the Browns rented a cabin on Whitefish Lake in the mountains. They drove there in a station wagon piled high with steamer trunks. Marilyn Brown had ironed and packed fluffy dresses for her little girls, but they ended up wearing jeans or swimsuits all during vacation. Julie remembers swimming without having had a formal lesson, "just doing it" after going into the water.

It was during these summer vacations that Julie's talent for running was first noticed. On morning jogs with Holly and their father, Julie ran way ahead of them. She ran back, then ahead again.

"She ran circles around us," recalls her dad. He also recalls how Julie would strike out ahead of the family on long hikes. When they made camp, Julie would sit apart, lost in her own thoughts.

"She was deep . . . right from the start," says her dad.

Back home in Billings, on Avenue F, Julie and Holly had lots of dolls but didn't play with them much. They played with their dogs—English setters and golden retrievers. They rode their bikes lickety-split. Their favorite stop was "Mom's Café," their kitchen at home where Mom kept lunch warm and cocoa hot. She called her active daughters "Heckle and Jeckle."

Then they were off again, for skating or marbles. Julie had no trouble winning the newest, shiniest marbles from neighborhood boys she played against. She outscored them in soccer and beat them in the President's Fitness Test at school.

"Kids would do sit-ups and pull-ups and they'd fall down exhausted," Julie remembers. "I couldn't understand what went wrong. It was so easy for me."

In classrooms Julie was less sure of herself—she was shy and quiet. Not because she found the work hard. She was a whiz at arithmetic. All her grades were good, even though entire days passed when Julie wouldn't speak in class. Not a word.

These silences puzzled and worried her parents. So when Julie was in third grade, her mother took her to the family doctor for some "chats."

The doctor sat behind his desk and asked Julie, "Is everything all right? Are you happy at school?"

Julie stubbornly refused to say a word.

"The more he tried to get into my mind, the more I closed up," she says now.

She had her own reasons, secret ones, for her shyness in school: she felt clumsy because she often fell down at recess, trying hard to win at sports. She also felt she looked funny because she was the skinniest kid in class. Looking good was important to Julie, even as a young child.

There was her hair, for example. If the part wasn't straight and her brown pigtails not braided perfectly, Julie tossed herself sobbing onto the floor.

And there were her ballet classes. Julie and Holly thought that dancing on tiptoes made them look silly. They hated to join the other dancers when the music began. Instead, Heckle and Jeckle sat giggling in a corner until they were both kicked out of class.

Julie smiled instead of cried every time she got spanked. No one was going to hurt her! She'd stay in her bedroom all day rather than admit she'd been wrong. In the evening her dad would come home and clear the air. A wise, soft-spoken man, the son of a lawyer and a lawyer himself, Rockwood Brown had the skills to make peace.

Both he and Marilyn had tried not to give Julie too much attention, tried not to spoil their youngest daughter. As a result, Julie had had to push to be noticed. She had to be different from her easier-going brother and sister. Soon, with two baby sisters added, Julie would be the middle child of five. She would need to strive even harder for attention. She would need to excel.

Julie developed an independent, competitive spirit within this large family. The family's loving support combined with Julie's physical talents to help her set world records in the years ahead.

2

Speed

In spring, each elementary school in Billings organized a track team. Girls and boys ran in the same races. Julie's specialties were the 50-yard and 100-yard dashes. She had little practice, except running a half mile to school each day. Yet she won all her races. This *natural* speed kept Julie winning at Lincoln Junior High School, where she and Holly were on the girls' track team.

In those days (1967–1970) running wasn't a popular sport in America. And running fast, except for short races, was considered "bad" for girls. Bad for their health. Girls were too weak! And bad because girls weren't supposed to be athletes like boys. It just wasn't right, most people believed.

Julie remembers that her training for races was more social than athletic: "At the track we'd stride one-hundred yards ten times. In between we'd just walk around and talk."

Julie still spent time riding horses after school. She had her share of falling off and being kicked, but she came back for more. Her dad had moved the family's horses, from the ranch he owned with his brothers, closer to Billings. Now Julie could take care of her own horse, Deuce, who had two white legs, and Deuce's baby, Ace.

She also had time for piano lessons and for work around the family's big new house. It sat under a rim of yellowstone, high above Billings. Julie helped plant trees in the yard. She repaired the lawn mower if it broke down. She tended her little sisters, Nancy and Becky. She cleaned her brother Scott's room in trade for rides on his motorcycle. Julie and Scott were great pals. He stood up for her in family arguments.

In winter Julie went skiing, which she'd picked up as quickly as her other sports. She'd simply watched her teacher when he'd said, "Follow me."

Every girl in the class, including Julie, had a crush

on him. They fought about who deserved to ski next to him.

With other members of her team, Julie entered ski races in Montana and Wyoming. "I raced recklessly," she admits. "I wasn't afraid of anything." In the season's final, she broke both skis. Her dad was so worried she'd hurt herself that he refused to buy her a new pair.

No matter. Spring had come—track season. Although still in junior high, Julie had been training with the Billings Senior High girls' team, the Broncettes. She'd been invited by Coach Phyl Miller to race the Broncettes at their workouts.

Julie beat them all, even the seniors.

Ms. Miller took running seriously. She didn't agree that it was bad for girls. With her help, Julie improved her natural speed. Julie did that by setting goals and training to reach the goals. She'd decide how fast she wanted to run a certain distance on the track. Then she'd train by running roads around Billings. She was so eager to improve that she ran much farther than Coach Miller required.

"Julie brought me the hub of an old wagon wheel one day. I knew how far from town she'd run to find it," Coach Miller remembers.

No one ever heard Julie brag about winning. As for any problems or complaints she had, she kept them deep inside.

Her high-school life revolved around her sports. In classes she earned good grades with little study. She attracted boyfriends without trying. She was chosen a candidate for homecoming queen in her senior year, but winning her championship race that spring meant more to her than being queen of anything.

She won the half-mile race at the Montana State Championships in two minutes, eleven seconds (2:11). It was the fastest high-school time, anywhere in America, in 1973.

Julie had grown from a skinny kid to a trim athlete, 5 feet 6 inches tall. Of those 66 inches, 41 were legs.

Her deep-set blue eyes now were fastened on her finish lines. Her brown hair flowed behind her as she raced. Every hair stayed in place!

"She moves like a fawn," some would say. Others described her as a lone wolf—and hungry.

After graduation Julie traveled to California for the Amateur Athletic Union (AAU) track meet, the most important track meet each year in America.

She went to the starting line an unknown runner. With little notice she took her place in lane three.

In lane one was Wendy Konig, who had been on

the U.S. Olympic team. In lane six was Mary Decker, *the* Mary Decker. Mary was only 15 but already famous for her speed and hot temper. Six other "name" runners waited for the start. Julie wasn't scared by them. Their best times for the half mile weren't all that much faster than hers. She knew she was well trained and well coached. And she loved to race.

The starter's gun fired, the runners sped their two laps around the track, and Julie won a trip to Europe!

She'd run 2:07 (two minutes, seven seconds), a personal record in the half mile. She'd finished fourth, good enough to get her on the U.S. Junior team. It was made up of runners under 20 years of age.

"I was proud to represent my country, thrilled to wear the U.S.A. uniform," Julie says.

That summer the team flew to Germany, Poland, and Russia. The U.S. Juniors won all their meets. They also had some spooky adventures. In Poland there were rats in their room. The Juniors stayed awake all night with the lights on, playing their portable stereos to keep from being bitten.

In Russia their hotel was visited by Russian Juniors. They weren't supposed even to talk to Americans, let alone hang around with them.

"They were so scared," Julie remembers. "One girl guarded the door. They wanted to swap their clothes for our Levis."

Julie came home to Billings without firm plans for college. *Her* choice was Flathead Valley Community College in Montana. She'd worked with the track coach there. Julie thought he could help lower her time for the half mile to two minutes flat (2:00). Speed and more speed was her main goal for the future. She wanted to go to Europe on other U.S. running teams. She wanted to set records.

Her dad thought Julie belonged at the University of California at Los Angeles (UCLA). There she'd have the chance for a wonderful education while she trained year-round in the sun.

"I practically had to tie Julie hand and foot to take her to UCLA for a visit," Rockwood says about his strong-willed daughter.

They walked around the campus. They had dinner with the women's track coach, Pat Connolly. Rockwood was impressed with Pat, a nine-times national pentathlon (five events) champion. But still Julie wouldn't give in. She had built up such trust in her Montana coach.

On the other hand, this past winter in Montana she'd run in bitter cold with plastic bags wrapped around her running shoes against the snow.

Julie chose UCLA sunshine for the sake of speed.

3

Distances

"I was so sure of her raw speed I'd've bet my house on Julie to win Olympic gold in the 800."

Coach Pat Connolly reached that conclusion after she had timed Julie on the UCLA track. Julie showed what she could do in the 100-meter dash, the 200, 400, and 800 meters. (Olympic distances are measured in meters rather than in yards; 800 meters is about half a mile.) Pat decided the 800-meter race was Julie's best distance. It combined Julie's foot speed with the endurance she had built in training.

Then, all of a sudden, Pat Connolly quit her job as

coach. She wanted more time at home. The job was given to Chuck DeBus, coach of the Los Angeles Track Club (LATC). A tense, handsome young man, Chuck was totally devoted to winning. He had begun to earn a reputation as one of America's best coaches of women athletes. His reputation was based on the many medals they'd won and the many U.S. teams they'd been chosen for.

Racing was becoming more popular with women. Sports doctors were pointing out that women's health actually improved with vigorous exercise. Women themselves now insisted on running in longer races, even in marathons. Their coaches and lawyers backed them up. So did the United States Congress. It passed a law, called Title Nine for short, that required colleges to set aside equal amounts of money for men's and women's sports.

At long last! Women could win athletic scholarships. They'd get their tuition, room, and meals free, or rather, in exchange for their time playing on college teams.

Julie Brown received one of the very first athletic scholarships for women.

Not that she needed it. Her grandfather Brown had left money for her education. But Julie deserved to be supported by UCLA in the same way their football players were supported.

She began her freshman year in September 1973. Her days seemed to settle into an ordinary cycle of classes and exams and part-time jobs and sorority parties and then more classes. But not really! Those were just the surface events of her life. Underneath lay Julie's real life, her emotional life—her running.

That fall she ran in cross-country races. She raced two miles, sometimes three miles. Chuck DeBus had moved Julie way up past the 800 meters. He didn't agree it was her best distance.

He says, "It was apparent from her workouts that she could run longer, faster, and stay comfortable. I wrote her a note."

You will be a finalist in the 1976 Olympics in the 1,500 meters.

He meant his note to inspire Julie. The 1,500-meter race (about a mile) was then the longest women's race in the Olympics. Chuck made for Julie a training schedule that called for running 40, 50, 60, 70 miles a week. She ran these on the UCLA campus and along the streets of Santa Monica to the Pacific Ocean and back. She ran the hills of Bel Air. She ran tree-shaded paths in Beverly Hills. Often the UCLA teammates ran together. Other days, Julie ran with Chuck or alone.

Speed is increased not only by running *long* distances at less than top speed but also by sprinting *short* distances as fast as possible. Several times a week Chuck met his team at the UCLA track. He held the stopwatch and shouted each second ticking away as Julie circled in 66 seconds, 65, 64. Even while sprinting, she moved smoothly, "almost like a cat," according to Chuck. She was so much faster than her teammates that there was little jealousy about her position as the team's star. She was as modest—silent—about her accomplishments as she had been in Montana.

For a college freshman, Julie had a fantastic cross-country season. She took third place at the AAU national cross-country race. This earned her a place on the U.S. team, which flew to Italy for the world cross-country championship. There Julie disappointed herself by finishing 27th.

"I was lagged out," she explains in athletes' slang. They mean they get hours behind in sleep by jetting across time zones.

She came right back for the spring track season. Each race she won scored points for the UCLA team. In some meets she ran four different distances. She helped her team take second place at the college championships by running the half mile, the mile, the two-mile, and finally a quarter mile of a relay race. Later in the season she set an American outdoor record in the three miles—16:08.

For many students, their freshman year, when they are freshly enthusiastic, brings greater success than their second year at college. Not so with Julie. She'd decided to major in kinesiology (say "kin-EES-ee-OL-o-gee"), which is the science of body movement. She kept up a B average in her classes.

Julie moved into a sorority house. She was known there as a caring, thoughtful "sister" who sometimes came late to dinner or missed it completely because she was running around—the track, that is! She was training for a spectacular year of racing.

During the winter she raced on indoor tracks. These were set up in huge basketball arenas. At Madison Square Garden in New York City Julie ran the mile in 4:43. She improved her time to 4:41 when she raced in the Russian-American indoor track meet in Richmond, Virginia. She enjoyed traveling.

Julie flew across half the world to race in Rabat, Morocco. It was blistering hot there for the world cross-country championship. She arrived several days early to make up for jet lag.

"All I did was sleep, eat, sleep, run a workout, sleep, sleep. I slept 15 hours a day before the race," Julie remembers.

The racecourse had been laid out on the infield of a horse racetrack. There were bales of hay to jump and rough dirt underfoot. A crowd of 10,000, including the rulers of Morocco, watched from the grandstand.

Julie went to the front of the race as soon as she could work her way through the crowd of 70 women. Then she kept them all behind her by pouring on speed. She surefootedly jumped the hay bales. She glided over the mud. Her footfalls were so light they scarcely left a print. She won the race and became the world champion, only 20 years old.

"It was just my day," she claims with modesty.

"She was confident for that race," says Chuck. And he should know.

One of the things coaches try to do with training is to bring runners to peak physical condition just before the race. They do that by gradually increasing the difficulty of each workout, then letting the runner

ease off and rest a few days. "Peaking" allows runners to race confidently, to pour on speed believing they won't run out of breath or energy. Chuck had peaked Julie perfectly for Morocco.

And by May 1975, Chuck had his entire UCLA team peaked for the college nationals. The year before, they'd been second in this same track meet, not good enough for Chuck. This year he'd used scholarship money and his reputation as a winner to get more and better athletes. Even at that, Julie had to run seven races in two days to help UCLA win. She won enough points to be the meet's high scorer.

"Hers was the best performance by an American distance runner I have ever seen in eleven years of coaching," Chuck told the few sports reporters at that track meet.

Women's running had yet to become a well-attended sport in America. It would be years before an audience would be built from those women now competing. They would eventually follow their favorite runners in the same way tennis players followed tennis stars.

Julie's teammates knew her value without reading about her in newspapers. She cheered for them at track meets. She joked with them at workouts. They in turn tried to cheer her up whenever she lost.

She took losing very hard. She'd go into dark moods

for days. But she'd never blame others for a loss. "I failed" was her attitude.

She had few losses until the summer of 1975. Then, as a member of the U.S. team, Julie toured Europe. She raced future Olympians. They ran aggressively, using their elbows to jab. They ran next to each other in tight packs, daring others to shove through them. Julie didn't jab or shove.

"I wish she'd been tougher," Chuck says. "She's always been such a nice person. She wants to be liked."

The East European women were rumored to be taking drugs, anabolic steroids (called 'roids for short), to help them run faster. 'Roids built bigger muscles than could be built by training. Also, 'roids helped muscles feel less painful after hard workouts.

Few athletes admitted taking the "little pink pills." Julie wanted nothing to do with them. Sports officials had decided that 'roids gave athletes an unfair advantage. Sports doctors believed 'roids caused cancer. It was certain that women grew hair on their faces from taking 'roids and their voices got deeper. Some women, however, were willing to accept these side effects and even to be called "cheater" in order to increase their speed.

The races Julie lost that summer were only small disasters compared to a virus she picked up in Russia.

It would haunt her running for the coming year.

Worse happened when Julie stopped for a visit in Billings. She got a phone call from Chuck. He stunned her with the news that he'd been fired.

4

Mountains

A winning coach fired?

At UCLA, where winning is everything, a battle tore apart the women's track team. Some members, including Julie, refused to compete unless Chuck came back. Others were glad he'd been fired. They had been the ones to complain about Chuck to the director of women's athletics. They'd said Chuck hadn't given them enough attention. Or that he'd given them too much attention. He'd pushed them to train too many miles each day. He'd screamed at them and made them cry. He'd told them they couldn't win without him.

Chuck had quarreled with officials at track meets. He bent rules to help his team win. For example, Julie had lost races because Chuck yelled advice to her from the sidelines. (Coaching during a race is forbidden.)

Chuck was not rehired by UCLA, so Julie now raced only as a member of his Los Angeles Track Club. She ran badly that winter of 1976. The Russian virus was sapping her strength. She had no spring in her step, no lift in her arms. She decided to drop out of school and spend her time trying to get into shape for the Olympic Trials. She'd have to run first, second, or third in her event in order to make the U.S. Olympic team.

Sick and weak from the virus, Julie ran fifth.

She went to the Montreal Olympics anyway, with her family in a camper van. Julie was sad and moody but never once threatened to quit running. She hurried back to California and transferred to Chuck's new school, California State University at Northridge, a town just over the mountains from UCLA. Julie's parents had urged her not to follow Chuck. They thought UCLA offered a better education. Julie had argued with them. She'd told them that she needed Chuck and she owed it to him to help build a new team.

And help him she did. She set an American record for the 5,000 meters (about three miles). She won the collegiate cross-country championship. And at Chuck's suggestion, she entered the AAU championship marathon.

Julie had never run a marathon.

Yes, but this would be only a workout, said Chuck. She could cruise it, not even break a sweat.

Julie gave in and ran. Chuck rode a bicycle beside her the whole way. He yelled, "Pick it up," about her pace. He wanted her to win, win, win. He yelled, "You look lousy."

"Get out of here," Julie answered. It was the first time she'd yelled back at Chuck. She felt pressured in this, her first 26-mile race. But she won. It took her only two hours forty-five minutes and thirty-two seconds (2:45:32) to become the AAU women's national marathon champion.

She won many more trophies that winter and spring of 1977, leading up to one of the great performances in American track history: Julie ran ten races in three days for her Northridge team. For those three days she was constantly warming up on the track's infield, then taking off her sweat suit and racing, then warming down, putting on her sweat suit, then warming up. She had no rest except at night. She had no chance to watch her teammates' events.

Julie could have chosen to run just one race and probably have set a personal record. But she unself-

ishly ran the 800, 1,500, 3,000, and 5,000 meters—semifinals and finals—to help her team against powerful UCLA.

Northridge almost beat them.

For this performance, Julie was named the Northridge Athlete of the Year. She was also named winner of two Broderick awards: one as the best college track athlete, the other as the best collegiate cross-country runner.

Julie went to Europe the summer of 1977 and specialized in the 800 meters. She ran a personal record of two minutes and seven-tenths of a second (2:00.7). Many of the European women were running the 800 in below two minutes. Julie realized she'd have to get faster to win at the Moscow Olympics in 1980.

Instead of faster, Julie got injured. And injured again. She twisted her right ankle during a workout in October. A month later she broke the same ankle. After ten days she ripped off her cast and tried to race. She favored her right leg. This caused a stress fracture of her left leg bone and of her right shin.

Julie raced anyway. She wore a pain-deadening device taped to her spine. She took pain-killing shots.

"She had a heart of steel," said track coach Tracy Sundlun, then of the University of Colorado. Other coaches felt sorry for Julie. They blasted Chuck for making Julie race.

Julie offered this in defense: "I've been told I don't have a mind of my own. Well, if it had been a knee injury where I could damage it for life, I wouldn't have run. Coach wouldn't let me. It was an injury that couldn't get worse."

Julie added in another interview, "I cry at movies. I'm emotional there. When it comes to physical pain, I don't cry."

Chuck arranged for Julie to spend six weeks of that summer at the Olympic Training Center in the Sierra Mountains of northern California. There she lived alone in a small cabin. She spent her days running on soft forest paths and working at a job she found for herself, wrangling horses. She dearly loved grooming, feeding, and exercising the horses. She guided riders to the tops of mountains.

She remembers a lame horse her boss wanted used daily to pay for its feed. Julie and other wranglers hid this horse rather than saddling it for the "dudes."

The Olympic Training Center had recently been founded to help Americans develop into world-class athletes. The tests Julie took there helped explain why she could run so far so fast. Her body weight of 107 pounds was only 6% fat. She had a maximum "oxygen uptake factor" of 76, which is a way of measuring the amount of blood that can be pumped by a heart per minute. By comparison, marathon gold medalist Frank

Shorter had been tested at only 71. Julie had 83% slow-twitch muscle fibers. Slow muscles are able to endure sustained work without getting tired.

She was a regular running machine.

And her six weeks of rest in the mountains had healed her injuries. She came down and won the Nike Marathon, setting a new American record while she was at it. Her time of 2:36:23 won her the Nurmi Award, given to the best woman marathoner of the year.

Julie was used to being the best. But she always wanted one more win. And one more. Even though she'd returned to Northridge to take biology courses needed for entering medical school, Julie kept her running career going strong. Being a sports doctor could wait.

She and other women now earned money by running. The sponsors of track meets and road races were awarding cash to winners. Shoe companies like Adidas provided free shoes and paid stars to wear them. Clothes companies paid runners to wear shirts, shorts, and caps with the company name in bold letters. This money was slipped to coaches to slip to their athletes, who were supposed to be amateurs. They were forbidden by AAU rules to make a living from sports.

Julie earned a small fee for being a runner in a

movie about Babe Didrikson (winner of two gold medals in track and field in the 1932 Olympics). Julie's fee and all her earnings went into a "pot" for Chuck's track club. In that way Julie helped support other women as well as herself.

She didn't really run for money. She ran to prove herself, and she especially loved to compete on difficult cross-country courses.

The 1978 fall season gave her a chance to race at AAU cross-country nationals against Jan Merrill, another outstanding American runner. Chuck made up a race plan that would beat Jan if Julie could stick to it. He knew Jan liked to lead in races. The racecourse had logs and gullies to jump, so Chuck said the leader would be thinking about each place she put her foot. She'd be telling her feet, "Be careful," not "Go faster!"

Soon after the start, Jan did take the lead. Julie stayed inches behind Jan, letting Jan's feet do the work of blazing a trail and letting Jan's body shield her from the wind. As front-runner, Jan was using more energy than the other 118 women in the race. Jan would be tired before Julie would be.

It takes mental toughness to stay in second place in a slowish race. Julie knew she could pass. But she held back. She waited and sprinted past Jan in the final meters of the race. Jan couldn't make up those few steps. Julie beat her by 2½ seconds.

"I like cross-country better than marathons," Julie told interviewers. She told others, "I enjoy the 1,500 meters best of all."

To tell the truth, Julie was uncertain as to what distance she should specialize in. If she ran only one distance, she'd be able to work on her tactics. She'd learn when to run in front, when to wait and pounce. Chuck believed she'd succeed best in the marathon, but there was no women's marathon in the Olympics. If Julie wanted an Olympic gold medal, she'd have to run shorter distances.

She ran lots of races, too many, according to Chuck's rival coaches. They gossiped that he was burning Julie out. They accused him of using Julie for his own glory.

If Julie had any doubts about her coach, she kept them to herself. She didn't grumble to teammates. She didn't give interviews except with Chuck by her side. She kept quiet and went to Puerto Rico to the Pan American Games in the summer of 1979 to compete against the best runners from North and South America. She won three silver medals, almost beating Mary Decker in the 1,500 meters. Julie ran that distance 4:06.4.

The Moscow Olympics were a year away. Julie would have to break four minutes in the 1,500 to expect an Olympic medal. Chuck decided she'd have to live at high altitude again to build up the hemoglobin content of her blood. Richer blood, high in iron, would make her stronger.

Julie went back to the mountains. Silvers weren't good enough. She wanted gold.

5

Trials

As the days of the 1980 Olympic Trials grew near, the U.S. athletes worried that they wouldn't be allowed to go to Russia even if they made the team.

The Soviet Union had invaded Afghanistan ("Af-GAN-iss-STAN"), a small country on its border. This caused President Jimmy Carter to threaten a boycott of the Olympics. If the Soviet Union didn't get out of Afghanistan, the U.S. team would stay home.

U.S. athletes reacted by writing letters to newspapers and to the President. Most athletes didn't want to see their training go down the drain, war or not.

They believed it was wrong and even stupid to mix sports and politics. Sports were supposed to be for fun. Other athletes supported Carter's boycott. They believed America should use any means to bring world peace, which was more important than gold medals.

The war raged on. Chuck DeBus kept his athletes in training. They were angry and depressed. But who knew? Maybe the boycott wouldn't happen. So they went to the Trials, where Julie placed second in the 1,500 and second in the 800. Her speed and persistence had finally put her on an Olympic team.

The Soviet Union continued the war. The team stayed home. Julie was bitterly disappointed.

President Carter tried to smooth things over with the U.S. Team by giving it a picnic at the White House. Julie wore her official team uniform, a cowboy outfit made by the Levi company. Her parents had come from Montana to be with her. The athletes were also honored at a program at the Kennedy Center, but Chuck scheduled a workout for the same time as this program. Despite her parents' asking that she attend with them, Julie did what her coach told her to do. She trained.

"I wish I'd put my foot down and insisted Julie go," Rockwood Brown says now. "I relive those troubled days in Washington all the time."

Julie flew on to Europe with the team, which would

be competing in summer meets *outside* the Soviet Union. She was peaked for a sizzling personal record in the 1,500, but it didn't happen. In her first race she tore her Achilles tendon (it joins the calf of the leg to the heel bone). She continued traveling with the team, hoping against hope to recover. She ended up wearing a cast for several months.

In the fall, Julie moved to San Diego to enroll there as a premedical student at the University of California. She was sticking with her plan to be a doctor, although she hated the sight of blood.

No one in the running world, least of all Julie, believed her racing career was over. She was just waiting for her leg to mend.

Meanwhile, marathoning was becoming wildly popular. Huge crowds now turned out to watch. Race directors gave thousands of dollars and new cars to the winners. Top runners could support themselves nicely by winning a few big races a year.

Popular or not, the women's marathon was not included in the Olympic Games. A committee of men had always been in charge of deciding on Olympic events. When voting against women's races, they had claimed there were already too many events. Why add another?

Their question angered women runners. The answer, of course, was that if men had the marathon, women should have it, too!

Led by Kathrine Switzer, a TV sports commentator who was a pioneer woman marathoner, women began to push for longer Olympic races. Julie herself worked for women's "running rights." The International Olympic Committee finally gave in and made the women's marathon an official event for the 1984 Games in Los Angeles.

Recovered from her leg injury in the fall of 1981, Julie went back into training. Chuck phoned from Los Angeles with her training schedule. Julie ran the New York Marathon in October 1981. She led for 14 miles on a pace that would have given her a world record. But she couldn't keep up her pace. She slowed, and finished ninth.

"I was too keyed up," Julie admitted. "I didn't hold anything back."

Her tactics were perfect, though, at cross-country nationals in November 1981. She "hid" in a large pack of front-runners until they all reached a narrow bridge near the finish line. According to plan, Julie spurted out of the pack to be first over the bridge. There no one could pass her. This gutsy move beat Mary Decker—and everyone else.

For seven years Julie had been America's most consistent winner in cross country, which is considered the most difficult form of running. She now hoped to become as consistent as a marathoner, for she had her heart set on making the U.S. Olympic Marathon team.

To gain experience, Julie returned to the New York Marathon in 1982. This time she ran patiently behind the great Grete Waitz from Norway, who was in first place. Near the end of the race, Julie made a move to be front-runner, but a tendon in her leg tightened up. She hung on to take second place. Later Julie confessed that the pain felt like a knife stabbing her leg.

That was Julie's last big race with Chuck DeBus as her coach.

Chuck and Julie had been winning together for nine years. Many in the track world were surprised by their sudden breakup. It wasn't really sudden. Julie had been quietly "growing" away from Chuck for several years.

"He was pushing me, and I was pushing me to win. The pressure became too great."

Julie found another coach, and she telephoned Chuck to explain. This call was stormy and difficult for both of them. When Julie put the phone down, she felt a mixture of relief and sorrow. Next she called her parents. They were "all for" the change.

"We felt Chuck had overtrained Julie," her dad says now.

Julie did not make a public statement until much later. She was shy with newspaper reporters, and they had learned to keep their distance. Eventually Julie revealed how she'd felt all along.

"I was eighteen when I went to UCLA, but emotionally I was twelve. I needed Chuck, but I gave him too much control. He told me when to eat, when to go to bed, who my friends should be. I found out when I was living alone in the mountains that I could make my own decisions."

Julie went to Oregon to work with her new coach. She was now the only woman runner of Bill Dellinger's, who coached the men's team at the University of Oregon. An official of Team Adidas had introduced them. Julie had been racing in Adidas shoes.

Dellinger was a low-keyed person, the direct opposite of Julie. He persuaded her not to compete so often. Fewer races might mean fewer injuries. Together they chose the Avon Women's International Marathon for her to run in preparation for the Olympic Trials. The Avon race would be held on the same marathon course that was going to be used in the L.A. Olympics. Running it would give Julie a chance to discover any kinks it might have.

Without pushing herself, Julie popped out front at the Avon race. She ran alone for the final twenty miles. At the finish line she had to wait seven minutes to say "hello" to the runner-up.

"It was boring out there by myself. But it wouldn't bother me at all to be that bored in the Olympics," Julie joked with reporters.

She wasn't bored with the winner's check of $15,000. She'd set a personal record of 2:26:24. This was the best time ever run in an all-women's marathon.

Coach Dellinger brought moderation to Julie's year of preparing for the Trials. She ate balanced meals. She had regular massages to help her relax. With the help of a psychologist, she practiced running the marathon in her mind. That way, she could correct mistakes before she made them. Julie baked her new coach a cake to thank him for her progress—his first cake from an athlete.

She arrived fit and confident in Olympia, Washington, for the Trials. At the starting line were the 238 fastest women marathoners in America. Before the starter's gun fired, a telegram from President Ronald Reagan was read over the loudspeaker:

"This historic moment certainly illustrates the great progress women have made in sports competition."

The gun fired.

The slower the better, Julie was thinking. Her plan was to use just as much effort as it took to place first, second, or third. She'd save herself for the Olympics, only twelve weeks away.

Julie let Joan Benoit get way out ahead. Cool and relaxed, Julie stayed in a loose pack. One reporter saw Julie smile on the course. At mile 8, Julie passed Coach Dellinger on the sidelines. He said nothing as she ran by. She passed him again where he'd moved to the sidelines at mile 18. There he cheered.

One by one, the women running beside Julie fell off her pace. She sailed to the finish and into the arms of her parents and sisters. Then the Brown family went to the parties honoring the first U.S. Women's Olympic Marathon Team: Joan Benoit, Julie Brown, and Julie Isphording. Champagne was served. Toasts were toasted.

Marilyn Brown remembers how outgoing and bubbly Julie was when people told her she'd win in Los Angeles. "They'd seen how much Julie was holding back in the Trials. They told her she was gold."

6

Watching Julie Brown

"Mother, I don't feel well," Julie said. "On the hill today I thought I wasn't going to make it back."

Julie had been phoning her mother often from the Olympic training camp at Santa Barbara, California. She described the runs she'd been taking in 110° heat. She was supposed to be getting used to the hot weather expected for the Olympics in August.

Marilyn Brown thought Julie's headaches might be nerves. But Julie's neighbors in San Diego were sure she had some sort of flu.

"When she left here she wasn't up to par," said a

neighbor who'd watched Julie run for years. A healthy Julie was easy to spot.

At the opening ceremonies the Brown family watched Julie march with her U.S. team into Los Angeles Coliseum for the lighting of the Olympic torch. The flame had been carried across America by runners. It had been sent from Mount Olympus in Greece, where the Games began thousands of years ago.

The flame would burn for 16 days and nights. Unfortunately, it did not signal that every country in the world supported the Olympics.

The Soviet Union and its friends hadn't sent teams to Los Angeles. They were paying America back for its boycott of the 1980 Olympics in Moscow.

The marathon would not be easier for Julie to win because of the boycott. The best foreign runners were not Russians. They were from Norway: Grete Waitz and Ingrid Kristiansen. Julie would have to beat them and her own teammate Joan Benoit.

Privately, Julie was worried about feeling tired and achy. But in public she spoke confidently. "My chances are good. I have as much ability as anyone else."

The day of the marathon was cooler than expected, only 75°. The race began on the track at Santa Monica College. Runners would leave the track through a gate, run the wide streets of Santa Monica, run south near the ocean, east on a highway, then climb a long, low hill to finish at the Coliseum.

There would be 2,500 marshals to handle the crowd of a million people lining this course. The race was also being televised to millions around the world. Not a bad audience for an event that had been forbidden women until this very moment: 8:00 A.M., August 5, 1984!

Julie looked troubled at the starting line and seemed not quite sure of herself as she ran the first miles. Back at the Coliseum, her family watched her on a gigantic TV screen overhead. She was in the lead pack. They'd be able to see her for the entire 26 miles—if she kept the lead. The Browns had only to wait and watch.

Joan Benoit soon moved into first place. The camera stayed on her, occasionally shifting to a small pack that fell farther and farther behind Joan. Julie was in that pack. A cooling fog swirled off the ocean, but it didn't seem to help her. Julie's face was tightening. Other runners picked up their pace, trying to catch Joan Benoit, but Julie fell behind the pack.

"Where's Julie?" her family began to wonder.

Joan had a big lead. The cameras stayed on her as she ran the freeway. Grete was in second place.

"Where's Julie?" Rockwood Brown asked with alarm when the camera swept back through the marathoners. His daughter had disappeared.

He left the Coliseum to look for her. There was

always the chance of terrorists on the streets, shooting at Olympians. Rockwood remembered the athletes who had been killed by terrorists at the Munich Olympics of 1972. He hurried to a first-aid station to ask questions. He felt Julie would have stopped running only if very seriously injured.

In the meantime Joan Benoit came running into the Coliseum. She'd won the race in 2:24:52. Grete Waitz finished second.

Runner after runner appeared on the track before Julie finally arrived. She moved slowly but surely. She was going to finish, even though it would have been less embarrassing to have dropped out miles ago. She came across the finish line, walked to the infield, and collapsed. She lay in a heap for 15 minutes, holding her head. Julie was crushed. Brokenhearted. She felt she'd let down her family and her friends.

After Julie left the field, her mother and sisters found her answering questions from reporters.

"We were crying like idiots," Marilyn remembers. Julie tried to be a good sport. In her own sweet way she comforted other runners who hadn't done well.

A few days later Julie drove to the mountains, alone except for her dog. Then she flew to her family's cabin on Whitefish Lake. Yet even at Mom's Café she didn't lose her tired, achy feeling. She ended up in a clinic, where blood tests solved the mystery of her 36th-place finish in the Olympic marathon.

Julie had a common virus—mononucleosis.

For Julie, there would be other seasons of running, new countries to visit, more friends to be made.

"As long as I believe in myself, I'll continue competing," Julie told her fans. She continued to train long hours even while preparing for a life outside the running world.

Julie changed her mind about medical school. She entered law school instead. She earned her tuition—and much more—by racing, by wearing Champion sports clothes and Reebok shoes, and by appearing in TV and magazine ads.

She raced in Japan, came home, and went again to train there part of the summer of 1987. This was a chance to work with a team again, to draw energy from their support.

The Japanese coach and his family lived in one corner of Julie's dorm. The track was right outside her window. There was also a covered track to use when it rained, and a weight-training room.

"I have never seen anything as nice as this in the States," Julie wrote friends. "The U.S. Olympic committee should come here and learn a few things about how to spend its millions to develop athletes."

Julie went back to Billings, Montana, for the Special Olympics there in 1987. Once again Julie wore her U.S.A. uniform. She started the torch run at Pioneer Park. She shook hands and signed autographs, and gave a speech to the young athletes:

"When I first started competing, my mom said it didn't matter if I won or lost. The important thing is to be out there trying. I realize now that Mom is pretty smart. Winners are people who are not afraid to try."

ABOUT THIS BOOK

There are competitive sports that leave you wondering how good you really are. Gymnastics, for one. And ice skating, diving, surfing. These depend on other people to decide if you *look good.*

In the sport of running, you never have to wonder. Good means fast, and speed can be measured. You can simply take a stopwatch to a track, run a quarter mile or marathon (105 laps), then compare your times with Julie Brown's.

I've done that. I've worked for years at speed. The hours of training that kept me from easy pleasures have taught me about Julie's grit. My own leg and lung pain taught me about the courage it takes her to run so much faster.

I've witnessed firsthand Julie's long life as a competitor. Since 1974 I've seen her run 100 races. Each has been freshly exciting. I've met her coaches and family. They and Julie have answered most of my questions. (She guards her training secrets!)

Better than words—I've raced against Julie. That's the nicest thing about road racing. Anybody can go off the starting line with world-class athletes.

You can, too.

R.R.K.